Steve Lavis

JUMP!

Ragged Bears

Tiger jumping,
frog jumping -
let's jump too.

Monkey swinging,
teddy swinging -
let's swing too.

I can't reach!

Lion roaring,
no one's snoring -
let's roar too.

ROAR!

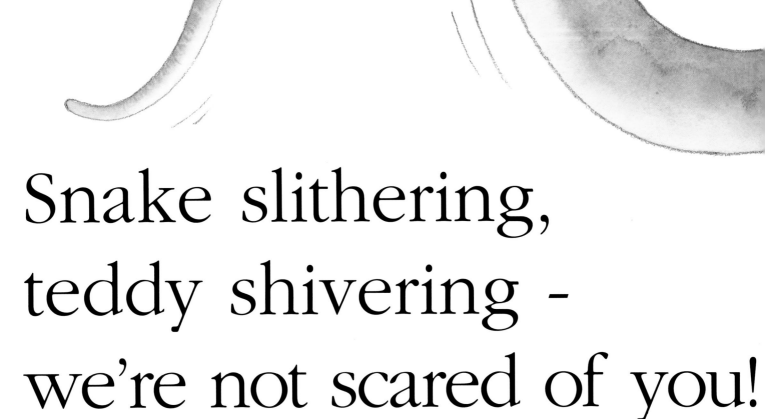

Snake slithering,
teddy shivering -
we're not scared of you!

Toucans flying,
frog trying -
teddy flying too.

Elephant stamping,
frog stamping -
let's stamp too.

Giraffe munching,
frog jumping -
we're as tall as you!

Crocodile snapping,
let's get clapping -
frog's scared of you.

Help!

Animals marching, monkey dancing - toucan flying too.

Lion marching, crocodile marching - let's all march with you.

STOP that marching, STOP that dancing - I've just shouted ...